Dedication

To my First Love, I am profoundly grateful for allowing me to dream again, for offering me new bloomed chances after the decayed ones, for seeing me as an ongoing masterpiece, and for enlightening me that I should love as You do.

To my Family and Friends, thank you for being my silent support system that is always there despite how bitter and sweet my season is, and for offering supportive energy during the days that my dreams and hope are occupied with darkness. Even without you being vocal, I know that you are proud of the person I become. Your silent presence turned out as the most comforting way of showing "You are not alone, and we are your home."

For every leaf that falls, this story would not exist without the person who once turned my dreams into ashes. It is also dedicated to him, so our memories will be immortalized through crafted imaginative words.

Contents

Wisdom   1

Sublimation   6

Special Day   12

Serving My Purpose   17

Broken   25

Reflection   31

Tragedy   38

About the Author   *46*

Wisdom

It's not enough that you wish to love and be loved,

You must know how to give and receive a love

that stays, communicates, and heals.

It is about taking good care of your heart;

it deserves better,

finds its peace when you don't settle for less.

MANY years passed, and I am here in our classroom, reminiscing on my past experiences, the good old friends, and the passersby who negated my worth and capabilities. The strangers I passed by in the street shouted at me, saying, **'Faggot'**, significantly my old yet gold version. I smiled gratefully out of nowhere, knowing that these experiences cultivated me to become the person I am now. An individual who walks with resilience, confidence and who consistently decides to stay faithful to his principles.

Being part of the third-gender community is challenging yet, grandiose. To walk and stand in this current generation, you must possess an enthusiastic voice that will speak for your authenticity and oddness. It also must contain bravery, tenderness, and not *just*.

With just a few months left, I'm about to take another step toward pursuing my purpose and conceiving the life I aspire to live in the future. I am all hands prepared to be a Psychology Student! But from now on, I have to remain in the conscious moment of being a grade 12 General Academic Strand student.

With time, I learned a lot of things. I'll never forget the lessons I learned from those realizations. You conceivably have friends who share some great leisure time with you and family who provide for your needs and love you unconditionally. But at the end of the day, the eternal truth is you only have yourself. *No one has enough courage to save you from life setbacks and suffering, but* **YOU** *can only do that.*

Things come and go so, as what people do, and yet sometimes, we forget to comprehend this as we are stacked in a particular situation; a situation that is simply hard to let go of, even though we are consciously aware of it, a situation that caused to forfeit ourselves though we were fighting it, a situation that we just wished not to be in there.

LET GO.

Yes, the solution is we have to let go. But the question is, *how to effectively let go?* How could I be able to let go if there is something inside me that says I shouldn't, and unfortunately, I cannot fight it. Saying let go is painless, yet doing it isn't. People who haven't been yet in that specific situation would never understand how it feels to have one. They might use defense mechanisms, but a liar spotter won't acknowledge them.

If we genuinely care for others, merely placing our shoes on them will be <u>a treasured help</u>.

"Hoy sister, why are you so tulala? Hindi fit sa 'yo ang pagganap kaya't stop that! You are not in the long drive to do that emote stuff. We have class, no. One more thing, baka ma-notice ka ni ma'am, you are not on the same page. It's your defeat if that happened," a lengthy statement Danica said. She gently tapped my right cheek to catch my attention to our class which kept losing due to my *'emote-emote thing,'* just like she said. That concerned and loquacious girl is one of my best friends.

"Begging a pardon, Mamu. I'm listening to the discussion even if I am tulala. I can multitask," I said in a whispering manner. Kapag nilakasan ko ang boses ko, there's a possibility that our teacher could hear me. Mayayari ang mga fersons. Nakakatakot pa namang tumingin si ma'am.

 P.s. *there are times na malakas ang pandinig ni ma'am. Be vigilant when she's your teacher.*

"Sure thing. I thought there was an unknown force that controlled you." She laughed without sounds. I merely gave her my white smile before reviving my attention on the discussion.

Ma'am Adriano is discussing business. Just like how to market your products effectively and that complicated SWOT analysis. I secretly idolize ma'am for being such an excellent teacher. There is a powerful aura in the way she speaks. A cup loaded with confidence for the way her body glances, the way she gives facts and information, and the way she throws jokes resulted in the class focusing more and chilling at the same time while learning.

If would not able to pursue Psychology, I will take Education. I think it is also my passion; to teach and inspire young minds who are hungry and thirst for knowledge. I will be delighted if luck selects BS Psych for me.

"Good morning, Ms. Adriano! May I take your time for a while?" A captivating female student outside the room interrupted ma'am from her discussion and asked permission.

Ngumiti si ma'am at lumapit sa pintuan ng classroom kung saan nakatayo ang estudyante na tumawag sa kan'ya. Sandaling tumahimik ang buong silid-aralan. Nag-recharge ang mga classmates ko ng kaunti para ma-absorb pa namin ang mga susunod na topic. Sabaw na ang mga utak namin ngayon sa dami ng impormasyon.

"Okay, class, that's all for today. If you have pending requirements in other courses, this is the appropriate time to do that as we have an urgent meeting. Catch you again in the next meeting," ang sabi ni ma'am nang makabalik siya sa table niya.

Inayos niya ang mga gamit niya sa lamesa at matapos ay tinawag kaming dalawang magkaibigan.

"Clever and Danica, paki-dala naman itong projector at bag ko sa faculty. Plus 10 sa formative assessment?"

Mabilis pa sa alas-kuwarto kaming tumayo ni Danica oras nang marinig ang additional 10 points sa incoming quiz. Napaghahalataang grade conscious. Pero joke lang ni ma'am iyon dahil parati niya kaming inuutusan.

Ma'am leaves the room which paves for the class to become wild. Kidding asserted. My classmates are all trustworthy and well-mannered. I belong to the first section. I am proud to be their classmate and class auditor. Yes! Even though I am not good at numbers, I was elected as an auditor of the class, though I love computing money.

Kinuha at inayos namin ni Danica ang mga gamit ni ma'am. Nang maiayos namin ang mga ito ay madali kaming tumungo sa faculty upang makabalik din sa classroom at gawin ang mga nararapat naming tapusin ngayong araw.

Morning pa lang, but it seems like a long day for me.

Will I still find the love I aim for a straight man? I'm not yet relinquishing hope since there is still plenty of time.

Sublimation

No one can heal loneliness,

reality holds power to do it

by tapping our soul that we don't need anyone;

to make us feel the blissful present

without worries about tomorrow.

to make us complete beings

who are <u>competent and worthy of doing everything.</u>

CLEVER had just woken up from bed when he heard the sounds of his pink alarm clock. This clock has sentimental value to him as it was given by his father before the accident that caused the death of his loved one. As time goes, it allowed him to heal the despair inside his heart.

Mabilis siyang tumungo sa kan'yang palikuran nang makita nito ang oras sa kan'yang personal phone. Ilang minuto nalang ang natitira para makapag-ayos bago tumungo sa paaralan. Kailangan na niyang magmadali. Oras ang pinakasagradong pag-aari na mayroon tayong mga tao.

Si Clever ang taong napakasipag sa halos lahat ng bagay, lalong-lalo na sa kan'yang pag-aaral. Nakatatanggap din siya ng lubos na pagmamahal galing sa kaniyang pamilya. Ang isang hiling nito, makatagpo din ng taong magmamahal sa kaniya ng tapat at tunay.

Clever

I have been scrutinizing this article for almost 4 hours, and my brain's appetite has now been fulfilled. I will spend the rest of the day having this word in my head; *Sublimation* is one of the defense mechanisms proposed by Sigmund Freud. It talks about choosing what is socially acceptable than doing the opposite when someone intrudes on your inner peace. This is what people nowadays must practice. It is a pathway to avoid doing unnecessary things and exclusively be efficacious.

"I have an entertaining and informative news for you that surely you'll love," biglang nagsalita si Danica na nakaupo sa tabi ko.

Tumingin ako sa kaniya nang nakakunot ang noo. "Oh, ano naman 'yon?"

Ours headquarter at the moment is the home of books in the school, researching ideas for prospective use. We are the archetype of persons who find wealth-accumulating academic thoughts to be functional dispensers of wisdom when our perfect time blooms.

"Lance, that's his name... Lance!" ang malapad na ngiti nitong sagot.

I paused for a minute to comprehend what she stated. Ah, I know! She's talking to that *straight man* I saw in our former building holding a Walis Tambo. Honestly, I started having an infatuation with someone. He is currently a grade 11 GAS student under the supervision of our former Adviser, Mr. Cruz. I cannot choose a perfect word to descriptively tell how my eyes perceive him and how my heart aims for his softest affection.

Maybe, my next move is to add him on his social media accounts? I have an idea that I can spark academic contributions to his life by helping him with his school papers. I am not sure if this would be a great way, yet I am still open-heart to giving it a try.

"Haler! Where did you get that information?" Ngayon lang ako nakasagot kay Danica dahil inuna ng isipan ko ang pagpalaot sa mundo ng imahinasyon.

"I have a lot of sources. Alam mo iyan!"

"Make sure that your resources are valid and well-fact checked!"

"Kahit putulin mo pa ang daliri ko at ipambayad sa utang niyo sa bangko!" ang matapang nitong wika.

Lance... what a fancy and joyous name.

"Aren't you gonna thank me for that?"

"I'll treat you later." Tinapos ko na ang usapan. Magtatagal pa ito kapag hindi ko siya sinabihan na ililibre ko siya ng pagkain.

Matapos ang mga oras…

'Bakla 'yan, pre. Tignan mo't dinaig pa ang alon sa paghampas ng bewang!"

"Halata nga, pre. Kapag natikman ako n'yan, tanggal ang kaartehan niyan sa katawan!"

"Iparanas mo nga ang isang nakahuhumaling na kaldag, bro."

I heard two people exchanging foolish conversations. I know; I am their hilarious topic as I am heading my way home. My older brother picks me up after school, but today I refused. I will not mind these people as I have this powerful word, *Sublimation.* I want to feel the presence that Earth gives me at this moment.

I've learned to manage my expectations of everything however, sometimes I forget these lessons. Like the kind of treatment of other people to you, you can't manipulate it, but we can choose our reactions over it. How sadness will instantly come on its own without even knocking at your door first and letting you know it so you can prepare. It will make you feel its power all of a sudden. How happiness doesn't arrive when we pray for it too. It will pretend it didn't receive the invitations we sent. Like us humans, it has a choice not to show up.

Every so often, we need to separate ourselves from all nonessential devotions to external things, if it's the passage through living a well-fulfilled life and experiencing the most authentic feeling of joy independent of any circumstances. If we retract our energy from the conscious moment, we unknowingly restrain ourselves from evaluating our purest intentions and embracing with tranquility all the opportunities the universe is sending on our paths.

I am always leaving my door open to readily acknowledge and hear stories that this world will let me have, either sad or happy. I will embrace whatever arrives first.

It's a privilege to educate yourself with the knowledge that could help you deal with these mean people. Sort of poor ones, not socioeconomically poor; hence, I tagged them as *intellectually impoverished*. Not having merely a cup of wisdom because they refused to embrace the fruit of education.

Some indigents will always be poor. There are plenty of things to desire, but some people chose to stay at places where even food cannot satisfy their starvation. Enlightened people are ravenous for success and happiness, while poor people crave edibles. See the difference? The other reason for this is we always mind what other people will say about us, so we do not try, or possibly, we feel purposeless or lack the energy to do things that can help us improve, in this case, passivity and doubt ate triumph wholely.

I am not saying these because I experienced them firsthand. I gathered the mistakes of others and devised them as approaches not to perpetrate the same things. That's why I always do my best in any circumstance in life. It is not an excuse if you are sick or tired. Making your best offers peace of mind. Setting it as your mindset will help you break the spell of guilt, blame, and self-punishment you have been battling.

Once I returned home. I did my things:

- ✓ Added Lance on his social media
- ✓ Reviewed our daily lessons
- ✓ Wrote motivational stories and prose
- ✓ Beauty rituals

Special Day

Sometimes, we disregard our happiness so we can spark light in the people around us. I discovered we can do both, imparting joy while being effervescent and fulfilled in accomplishing it. Some people counterfeit their identity with others, pretend to have a good soul, and have good skills in camouflaging their reasons for staying in your life. We don't deserve this kind of people. We want people who value integrity and good work even when alone, even if no one is watching.

Clever

LANCE and I started to have a virtual conversation. It was not mutually decided; I was the one who insisted on making it happen. I should not spark actions like that, yet some natural forces let me do so.

After five weeks of talking on social media platforms, my ever-supportive friends created a way to cross paths personally. It was on my special day. I was glad as I never assumed I could experience a surprise birthday from them and Lance, who served as my galaxy that day. My mind indicated possibly he was the man I had been searching for since then. Was I persuaded? I knew I was.

This particular day is finally on the list of treasured events in my existence. What made it remarkable were my authentic happiness I felt that day, and of course, *him* to be added to the claim. God indeed blessed me with good friends who support me in any way possible.

Last day, Lance asked me to make him a speech for the school's pageant he would be joining. The pageant aims to help promote and conserve our mother earth. Since I felt tons of butterflies start crawling on my tummies, it was my pleasure to be trusted to write one for him.

As a result, I did everything to make him win the contest, yet he must accomplish his part to attain that goal. He's honest with me, as he voiced out that he is shy and does not intend to win the contest; his adviser and classmates just pushed him to be the representative of their strand. Above all, I'll still give him support in any form.

I have shown care, support, and trust in him. To analyze these things more deeply, we can conclude that it's a service of love. I am begging for love, his affection. I am consciously aware of it. After a long scrimmage, it went deeper that could kill a glimpse in my eyes if he left.

'Hey, pagawa naman ng short story for 21st century literature. Need na kasi ipasa bukas.'

I'm presently in front of my Laptop proofreading my electronic journal for Philosophy class. I was about to let my mind and body rest, but an urge entered my consciousness when Lance's message appeared on the screen.

Here him again, giving me work to do. I have functioned as his instructor every time he has requirements in school. I also shared with him my strategies to get high scores in exams. I hope he will bear that in his mind.

I replied, '*okay*'. Hindi naman 'yan matamlay para sa matagal na oras na paghihintay.

It's already 11:50 PM. An irony of this, I've been waiting for his message since we left each other's presence after school. Bakit ang tagal niyang 'di nakapag-online? Ano ba ang pinagka-busy-han ng isang ito? Sa totoo nga niyan, nakagawa na ako ng malayang prosa habang nakatulala sa taas ng aking puting kisame.

Kung dumating ang pagkakataon

na makasalubong mo ang dilim,

'wag kaligtaan na ang pangalan ko ay banggitin

susubukan kong alisin ang takot

at pipigilan ang hayag nitong bangungot.

Sa oras na hindi mo na makita pa ang daan,

Tanganan mo ako,

iaalay ko ang natitirang liwanag na naririto sa dibdib ko.

Ibibigay ko ang lahat,

kagaya ng kandilang handang maubos,

huwag mo lang maranasan ang unos.

'Anong oras na! Saan ka galing? Bakit ngayon ka lang nag-chat? Matulog ka na. Kay hilig mong magpuyat kaya pinagkakaitan ng taba 'yang katawan mo.'

Mensahe ko sa kaniya na tila isang magulang na pinapangaralan ang pasaway niyang anak.

'Sakit naman ng pinagkaitan.' He sent this using voice message. Puwede ko na bang sabihin na kaya akong palutangin ng boses niya sa alapaap?

'Gusto mo pagkaitan din kita ng oras ko? At hindi ko gawin ang activity mo para maramdaman mo ang mapait na parusang hatid sa mag-aaral na kagaya mo?' ito naman ang aking ni-reply sa kan'ya.

'Kakayanin ba ni Clever na ipagkait ang katiting niyang oras sa cute na kagaya ko?' He sent me his cutest selfie.

Clever, hold yourself. Huwag kang kikiligin. Everything is normally happening. I passed my kilig on the pillows near my left fist by squeezing it femininely.

'Oh, saan ka nga galing?'

Birthday kasi ng pinsan ko, nagkayayaang uminom. Hindi naman ako lasing. Kakauwi ko nga lang. Matutulog na sana ako kaso naalala ko 'yung activity namin. Hehe! Ikaw, bakit gising ka pa?

Ito ang valid reasons niya? Bakit hindi ka nagpaalam sa akin? Paano kung may mangyaring masama sa iyo? Wala akong kaalam-alam! Ano nalang sasabihin ng mga kaibigan at pamilya mo sa akin? Pabaya akong girlfriend? Tinuktukan ko ang sarili ko dahil sa pagiging hibang ng isip ko. Masyadong nagpapadala sa ritmo ng marupok na puso.

I clicked that sleep command on my Laptop to focus my attention on our conversation. I am also done with my activities. It's time to satisfy my ego again. We talked for 2 hours while I was doing the activity. When it passed, he finally closed his eyes and started to gain energy again. I sent him *candy dreams* and sweet, *beautiful nightmares.*

Lessons I learned this day,

Humans have different levels of moral reasoning. Some Philosophers do not examine what you do but the motives behind those actions. There are certain areas in our lives when we are placed in situations where it will assess our moral principles. Even so, universal laws and care for all living things should reign in this world.

I am starting to be surrounded by the love I have sought for a straight man. I'll fight consequences merely to experience how to be loved by a man I am destined for. I will embrace and enjoy every bit of it and take the necessary action when it arrives.

Serving My Purpose

Since then, I have heard stories of broken promises,

betrayal, and damaged relationships.

I wonder what causes these things to happen;

maybe, one of the reasons is that we are surrounded by stimuli.

Some chose to respond in ways;

that violates rightful principles

and traumatizes someone's heart.

Clever

YESTERDAY, I thought it will be part of my casual days passed without something that thrills me happening. The whole day might not go well, but there's something good that happened that day. My phone rang. This sent me an event that I should prepare for. My soul's partner called me and tried to have my permission if our eyes could gaze at each other physical aura once more.

"Kita tayo bukas."

This line written of three words might perceive by others as a standard message, but for me, it means the world. Is there a thing invading Lance's mind right now? He has been acting differently lately. I must trust my intuition as it tells me this will be a romantic meet-up.

Today is Friday in the afternoon, just get done taking our entire midterm exams for the second semester. The questions prepared by our teachers were so out of this world. You will be put under ordeal to determine if you spent days and sacrifice certain unproductive habits to review the coverage of the exam indicated in the table of specifications which was given a week before the midterm examination begins. Deep in my beating heart, I did my best and hoped for high grades.

Mag-aasam ka nalang, iyong matayog na.

My conscious mind tries to forget what Lance said to me last night; hence I am here in our classroom waiting to capture his presence. I don't want to tell my friends about spending time together. I know it's not an intimate date, though when you ask what my heart felt, how I wished it would turn like that.

Ms. Angel, our subject teacher in Technology Literacies, is sharing deep conversations about particular faith in life in our classroom. She was merely bored at the faculty. I might say that we are biased students. Some of my classmates are not here anymore. I think they also want to enjoy the precious remaining time after our knowledge has been squeezed up by the tests.

Ma'am Angel said that this religion is the best among all because her soul connects to what it believes. She experienced being in another religion; hence truth prevailed, she was not fulfilled, and there was a blank to be occupied. Ma'am felt how painful it was to be judged by her family for the philosophical beliefs she chose to hold. Nevertheless, she persists in standing for what provides her fulfillment and glorifies her soul to continue living and do better for her home and fellow human beings.

I am a Catholic, although I sometimes get confused about where to believe. Maybe I got influenced quickly when other people talked about their beliefs. I put trust in my phases that someday, I will be in a situation wherein I no longer have to torture my mind with questions that I do not have enough knowledge and experience to give a solidified answer. The holy creator will bless me with light to see the bloomed path to take.

After our loving teacher shared her experiences, I checked out my messenger, and there was a special message I always wait to see; his message. I am amidst being excited and nervous to open the message. It's time to put some magic on myself to look presentable to him.

"Mukhang mali si Ms. Nora dahil may himalang nangyayari ngayon! Bakit nagpapa-ganda 'yarn? Saan ang awra?" Nagulat ako sa lakas ng boses na ibinuga ng bunganga ni Marco- my gay man best friend.

"Secret. Hulaan mo!" Tumawa ako ng medyo malakas habang patuloy ang pagpahid ng mabagong pulbos sa aking malambot na pisngi.

I refused to state the truth. I want to surprise my friends once Lance arrived at our place to pick me up. Lance arrival will be the departure of uncertainties on their minds.

"We're not born yesterday!" My best friends shouted at me this. Shabay-shabay talaga sila? Choir kayo, girl? Ang alam ko tapos na ang speech choir competition sa school, ngayon pa lang sila nagpapakabihasa? Kidding aside.

"What you think about me is not my business to handle anymore." I ended the conversation with a bang as I just love leaving conspiracy. Let your loved ones be wondered at times.

Some stories must remain unspoken; keeping them as secret is the way to protect what remains, things no one holds power to invade.

Lance's Cave

I and Lance are now here at the place where he currently stays. His home is located far at the school so he needed to live during weekdays on her auntie. Naawa ako sa kan'ya nung sinundo niya ako sa room dahil pawisan ito at gusot ang suot na uniform. Sila raw ang nakatalagang taga-linis ng buong silid-aralan. Katulad ng kung ano ang inaasahan, nagulat ang mga kaibigan ko nang makita si Lance. Mahaba ang tuwid at rebounded na buhok ng kaibigan nilang si Clever, wala akong magagawa.

I want to serve my purpose today to assist him in finishing his pending school papers. He confessed that he had a project to do. He will not receive a grade in one subject if he cannot pass it on Monday. He is alone at the place. His cousin returned to their birthplace after the exam, and her auntie is currently at work.

"My highness!"

Napasigaw ako nang hindi inaasahan nang makita ko ang ginagawa ni Lance. He is taking his uniform off. My eyes are starting to lose their virginity. Help me. I am not even conscious of how hot his body is. Not so fit, but that's the built I desire. I quickly managed my expressions to act decently and respect him.

"Just enjoy your scenery. Hindi ka na iba sa akin," ang wika niya nang nakangisi.

Pumikit ako at hinagis sa kaniya ang yellow paper sa tabi ko. "No, not this time. Maybe, bukas!"

Seven In The Evening

'NASAAN ka? Gabi na! Busy pa rin sa school?'

Masyadong akong nag-enjoy sa ginagawa namin. Hindi ko na namalayan pa ang kasalukuyang oras. Bumalik ang diwa ko nang mag-text si mama. I can't grasp the surrounded emotion sa text ni mother. Baka galit na siya dahil anong oras na rin. I replied her reasons correspondently to focus again with our business.

Our set-up is this, I'm typing in front of his computer, and he's sitting at my right side, sparking moral support.

"Ganito ba?" ang tanong niya. Ang utos ko kasi sa kaniya ay imasahe niya ako sa likod para mawala ang back pain ko.

"Make it smooth," ang hiling ko. Lalaking-lalaki ang pagpiga niya sa likuran ko. Baka bago ako makauwi niyan, wala na akong likuran. Charis!

"Boss ba kita?" ang tanong niya. Hindi ko inaasahan na kikilitiin niya ako sa batok ko.

Eh... sa tingin ko, kailangan ko siyang bigyan ng pananakot.

"Titigil ka or titigilan kong gawin ang project mo?"

Daig niya pa ang naka-programang machine dahil agad na hininto ang kaniyang ginagawa.

"Sabi ko nga, master kita." Sumuko siya na parang batang inagawan ng laruan. Hindi naman makati ang ulo niya pero napakamot siya rito. Pinagpatuloy ko ang ginagawa ko hanggang sa mapahinto ako dahil sa malalim niyang tanong.

"Kung makakapagsalita ang bukas, ano ang sasabihin mo sa kaniya?"

Tumingin ako rito at saglit na nag-isip. Huminga ako ng malalim bago sumagot. "Make me as an eraser, so

I could undo my mistakes. Thank you for making me realized I don't need to mourn every night when I see the moon, I know the sun will be back, I need a love that feels consistent and sure."

Binigyan ko siya ng ngiti. "Ikaw?"

Ngumiti rin siya sa akin bago sumagot. "Hugutin mo patalim ng mga ala-ala niya sa paraang hindi ito mag-iiwan ng sugat sa kasalukuyan."

Tagos sa puso. Kahit ganoon ang ngiti niya, ramdam ko na may bibit itong pait.

Maya-maya lang, I heard that odd sound his tummy produced, a sign of starvation. "Gutom na ako, let's continue it later." He's honest.

"Instant noodles at hotdog lang katapat niyan!"

Lumipas ang mga oras. Dumating ang pagkakataon na kailangan naming muling iwan ang isa't-isa.

My fingertips are dealing with difficult times, picking artistic phrases to make the world know how delighted I am now. I am immensely grateful for the abilities that God has granted me as I use them to give peace of mind to this person who shares my heart peace.

I made Lance's dessert and cooked dinner, having some normal conversation before deciding to send me home using his aunt's spare car. Some people will say that he's just treating me like a friend and not more than that. However, they cannot ever read and understand the messages it's sending to me.

Regret only comes in the end,

it is a nightmare of the opportunities we took for granted,

yet it is not scary as the nightmare

that visits you when you're sleeping,

this one sparks hope and reflection

grab the opportunities you met along the way

<u>let your dreams have a soul and be tangible.</u>

I can't deny the voice in my head that says; *I am solely tolerating Lance's actions.* As we continue sharing time, these fuels which sustain my burning fire toward moral principles are retracting piece by piece by the moment itself.

Broken

When someone makes you feel unwanted,

unheard, and underappreciated,

don't depart to make them feel sad

walk away as you can no longer grasp the reasons for staying.

In these times,

you have to be resilient enough to stand up for yourself,

remember,

what is meant to be will, and what is not won't.

Clever

'ALWAYS *choose yourself whatever happens.'*

A super-random text was sent by Danica before I closed my eyes last night. People nowadays are behaving differently.

Choosing yourself will make you happy for sure. But this question intrigues me, what drives people to be truly happy? Does it come with possessing material things or being found within a person? Seeking happiness can lead you to battle your mind to ascertain what profoundly occupies it. Sometimes, a stimulus rises and slaps us straight in the face so we can open our eyes to reality; *we are not happy.*

People might be smiling, yet authentic happiness is missing.

Is there no good or bad thing when it comes to happiness? How can you exemplify when what offers you satisfaction will not be proper for others? Confusion takes me. I already authorized it to control a portion of steps in my life.

Maybe, loving makes us happy. Happiness and love are inseparable. So, why do we love? As for me, simply because we are allowing ourselves to have chances to be happy and experience what some say is a *Happy Ending.*

I disagree that love always brings a Happy Ending; sometimes, it gets an *Undying Ending;* even if it ends, pain is still living- colonizing your existence and slaughtering your heart daily. It might not bring a Happy Ending, but indeed, it will create redirection and rediscovery.

Our semester ends, and sorrow begins.

Book Store is my relaxing hideaway right now, hunting for books about Introduction to Human Psychology and related topics. Another update for the events added to my story, I will be taking an entrance exam at a well-known private university here in our town this coming September. Added to my cravings is to pass their scholarship program so I could pamper myself with books once I get the financial assistance. No kidding, as I would do that.

I am with myself, I invited Danica to join me, but she is committed to attending a bible study for the youth community she is part of. I am alone but not lonely. I value being alone as it offers me a substantial opportunity to be who I am. I would do things alone rather than be in the company of fake people.

If you dare to ask me if I invited Lance, my answer is we have not talked again for almost *three days* since this academic break began. I think he's busy because he didn't even pour a few seconds to tap that thumbs-up button to let me know he still exists. I always see that green small circle thing which means he's online whenever I message him. I gave bunches of messages and calls but received nothing in return.

His silent action makes me hate myself for caring a lot, but I need to act like I am not affected. Ano kaya talaga ang rason niya kung bakit hindi niya ako nire-replay-an? I just remembered what Marco frankly said to me a day before yesterday.

"Kasabay ng pagtatapos ng semester ay ang pagwawakas din ng komunikasyon niyo. I thought, you're good at making hypothesis but common sense has left your brain. Bakasyon, no requirements to do, move on, dahil wala ka nang role sa buhay niya. As easy as that, girl!"

I know Lance more than the eyes of Marco. I am too fooled as I can hardly accept his theory that Lance was just using me even though I have sensed it. It's more painful to say these words to yourself than to hear them come from other people's mouths.

Should I conclude that it is a good indicator that you must know someone for a long time before falling for that person deeper? Kapag nawala siya, maiiwan kang nakakulong sa nakalulugmok na paraiso.

The grandiloquent moments and beautiful times we had together are endless. This makes my heart paralyzed. Hearing his name and seeing his angel face can heal its decaying life and revive its beating power.

Cursing to imply that I love him. As I always tell myself, I am not yet fully equipped to face what will happen next to our chapters- how huge are the stone we have to carry on our paths.

Fleeing to the stars that Marco's conspiracy is not valid. Please, Moon, tell me what to do.

"Excuse us."

A circle of friends asked for some space. This drove me to get in touch with reality. I smiled and gave them a conducive space.

"Have you heard the chismis?" one of them speaks.

"Spill the tea."

Not included in social etiquette is listening to strangers talking, so I didn't mind them not until I heard the following lines.

"I saw Lance and Kayla earlier at the music store. Are they being intimate again?"

The moment my ears scented that name, something puzzling entered my heart delivering confusing pain due to Lance never shared me about his love for music. At the same time, he was not the only man on Earth with that name. To be sure about my claim, I walked closer to their side.

I made myself busy pretending that I was not listening to their conversation.

"Based on what I know, Lance has been courting Kayla for almost 2 years since our Junior High."

I can't even gaze at the aura of the speaker; my position is on their back. After hearing this information, I decided to pay for my selected books and forget what I just listened for, still unsure about that.

Starvation brought me to a pastry house and convinced me to pamper myself with some desserts. I merely expected I would only be seeing sweet delicacies; even so, my eyes unexpectedly captured two people who can be termed as couples for their position and motions.

After seeing this live event, my fragile heart couldn't hold itself anymore; the heavy emotions ripped it. Before my eyes pour their tears, grateful to my mind as it says, *"You have to walk away as you have no safe space in this place."*

I didn't even think twice about following what my mind stated. I composed myself and stood as if nothing had happened. I got out of the place and decided to let this pain take me to a place that truly belonged to me- a place I could call my *silent sanctuary*.

My claim has been validated. It's Lance flirting with a girl in front of me. I hope he did not notice my presence.

The greatest lesson my mom taught me when my dad left… all people in your life will have a departure. You, yourself, even if you have owned that person for a long time, can't tell when will be their last day. It stabbed me right now.

There will be someone who will say that they love you,

but they don't literally love you for who you are,

they just seek the concept of how they feel about themselves because of your love,

or they love what they can take from you.

Reflection

Love is worth fighting for
yet sometimes,
you can't be the only one fighting
to still be worth it to pursue.
There are times
that people need to fight for you too
and if they don't,
it's time for you to move on and reflect,
what you're giving them
is way more than they are all hands to offer.

Clever

TIME accompanied me to my preferred spot, where I go whenever sorrow and pain attack me. This shelter is my comforting refuge, where I contemplate my actions, decisions, and motives. I don't need to engage my family or friends in this dejection in which I am the culprit. I can handle this one bravely and intelligently. I trust it has enough paddles to get me passed this drowning wave. I have to release some air; this is just a detour of my journey.

Long before you seek something,

you already have it,

take a look at your life,

make time to have a peek within.

It doesn't matter anymore if Lance saw me or not. The event opened my mind similarly not to be dependent on him or anybody else, especially regarding my happiness and validation. I cannot explain the intangible drug Lance let me sniff; inconsolably, I become addicted to him.

I am informed about this, but walls are built and it lessens my power to admit what my instinct says. Perhaps, we sometimes need to sugarcoat what's happening in our lives. We must ware a solid blanket to protect ourselves from living in reality because it profoundly hurts. We have to set aside that these are just comforting lies, some sort of temporary safety.

The first time I fell in love with another guy aside from my brothers and late father went not smooth as the academic achievements I attained these past years. I'd say that it brought fragileness not to confront my Id. However, things in life will always arrive at their ending. No matter how long the journey will be, it has an endpoint. This let me burn the characteristics and perceptions I maintained that are no longer helpful this time.

I pledge myself that this is the beginning of my healing journey. As much as I want to leave all these tears here, I can't do that. I can't escape the process of reinventing and relearning to treasure my existence again. Healing the tore pieces inside me will take time. It's not just a one-sitting process. It's difficult to rebuild things if the foundation has cracks.

Only time can tell if all the wounds are gone and turned into beautiful scars.

I miss the genuine smile I used to have before searching for a straight man just to prove that I was worthy of love. Perhaps the moon is tired of watching the dramatic and fake story that Lance and I are making.

Once a particular thing passed, we should move on and continue walking. Tandaan, ang buhay ay parang gulong, umiikot, kaya't nararapat lamang na magpatuloy. Huwag hahayaan na ang gulong ay mananatili lang sa isang destinasyon at hindi na patuloy na aarangkada pa. All things are temporary. Even Earth, I know will be gone, years and years from now.

New Semester Begins

"Puwede pa naman tayong maging *magkaibigan*, ulit."

I let chance take part in my life again with limitation. Putting limitations on my actions and expectations will guard me against experiencing yesterday's nightmare. I have freedom of choice, but it requires **self-control**. If I don't build boundaries, it will affect my being. That's why laws were formulated to control people's behavior. Hindi lahat ng gusto natin ay maaaring makuha at hindi lahat ng kaya nating makuha ay tama at makabubuti sa lahat.

 I offered all my ears to listen to his narrative. I quickly forgave him as I could connect to his reasons and explanations. Instead of arguing about who is wrong and who is correct, we talked about what is right and what is wrong. I acted like a real woman who expected a straight man will love me. That's my fault, yet the lessons I received from it radiate from the pain itself.

Set of new realizations about *Faith* and *Love*.

I thought the universe had forgotten me and God was not ready to give me the right person who was willing to be on my behalf. I took the meaning of love that vague. I thought love could be forced and begged.

Fall in love with yourself first. Be willing to be your own soulmate. The affection you are seeking for someone is the manifestation of the desire to know yourself completely. I know it's pleasurable to see yourself more kindly through the lenses of someone else, but the same way you're longing to be loved is the way to love the strength and fragileness within you, to fall in love deeply with your capabilities, to look after yourself day by day, to hear the vivid sound of your approval, to get a little dream you can be proud of. Until you are on your behalf, you will have the courage to stop asking others to fill the needs they were not born to meet.

Almost all my closest friends, especially Danica and Marco, noticed the change in my attitude and behavior, but they are happy with how capable I am again in life. Lance continues to impart butterflies to that woman, Kayla. They will be in a relationship soon. I wished all the best for him because I loved him, and I still do. Perhaps, it makes us bolder if we let go.

'I love you, even if you love her.' What an eight words short story.

Habang abala ako sa pag-aayos ng study table ko dahil nabasag kanina iyong alarm clock na bigay ni dad, hindi ko inaasahan na tatawag sa akin si Lance. Tinigil ko muna ang ginagawa ko upang masagot ito, at makausap siya.

: Hello?

A minute passed after answering the call, but I heard no words said by him. *Bakit ang tahimik?* I feel something strange even though I am not with him.

: Hey?

I spoke for the second time. This time, I heard a cry. I know where it came from.

: Oh, anong nangyari? Umiiyak ka ba?

Mga pinoy talaga, alam nang umiiyak. Tinatanong pa. Dapat ang tinanong ko ay kung ano ang dahilan kung bakit siya umiiyak.

; Nag-away kami. Tapos na ako.

Nag-away? Sinong kami? Sila ni Kayla? Bakit parang kanina lang ang saya-saya nilang dalawa? Should I ask what happened? Narinig ko ang malakas na pagbusina sa kabilang linya.

: I'll listen; you have me.

Ito nalang ang nasabi ko.

*; She's a piece of shit! My cousin got her pregnant. They made me a f*cking shit.*

This line provided narrative description behind my man's cry. Hindi ako naka-sagot simply because I'm out of words. Bilang babae, ito na marahil ang isa sa pinakamasakit na magagawa mo sa lalaking nagmamahal sa iyo, ang mabuntis ka ng ibang lalaki, sadya man o hindi.

; Kanina ko lang nalaman but I've seeing the changes sa katawan niya before…. dahil sa inuman kaya nangyari 'yon. A-ang tagal ko siyang hi-hinintay, Clever. Pinsan ko lang pala makakadali sa-sa kaniya. Sobrang sakit… da-daig ko pa sinaksak ng paulit-ulit.

The occupying emotion in his words created knives that kill me triple than what he feels. I want to offer him something that can help to ease the sorrow he feels right now.

: Don't even think of anything that could harm yourself, okay? Where are you? Gusto mo bang puntahan kita ngayon?

If my presence could help easing his pain right now, pupuntahan ko siya kahit saan. Kahit magkaligaw-ligaw ako, maalayan ko lang siya ng kalinga ko.

; Hindi mo na kailangan mag-abala. Kaya ko na 'to.

What a projection, indeed. He tried to use reverse psychology on me so I would stop asking him. He's drowning in emotions. He needs my arms as I can feel it.

: Nasaan ka nga kasi?

Doble ang pag-aalala ko dahil alam kong naka-inom siya at kasalukuyan siyang nagmamaneho ng sasakyan. Ang kulit nitong si Lance.

: Hoy! Tinatanong kita? Nasaan ka?!

Ang tanong kong muli gamit ang mataas na boses. Sinamahan ko na ito ng dasal na sana totoong may mahika, haplusin nawa nito si Lance at gabayan na makauwing ligtas.

; Pauwi na ako, Clever. Magpahinga ka na.

This is the last sentence my ears heard from him before he ended the call.

Tragedy

Even up to these days,
I cry often
I still do as I miss you,
it's tearing my heart,
poisoning my mind
because I can't define what I am missing,
a lot of good things to think about you
I know it's not the concept
or role that I can't let go of,
it's solely you that I am always thinking of,
I hate that you're gone.
For the love of God,
I can't find another you,
someone who can fill the spaces you left
they can recreate all your steps,
the things that make me flow in the clouds
imitate things that make you unique,
every bit of atom that makes you shine

but they can't be you,

they are not like you,

and what I want is you,

not anyone else.

Clever

"SMILE."

Here we are, visiting the man that I first loved in my life. The first ever man who was there when I hailed in this world, who supported me all the way he could, and who ignited the fire of resiliency within, yet fact has to be said, he's also the man who made my feet broken and be vulnerable when he chose to be with God and left us.

Being left with someone you love the most is like killing half of yourself every day, and no amount of treatment or medicine could be in assistance to temporarily cover the pain. It's like living in a nightmare while your eyes are wide open and the moon's light is much brighter than your path. Years passed, but the pain hasn't yet healed; it stays, *and I just learned to live from it.*

We all deserve forgiveness for allowing ourselves to have a new beginning.

May you offer the forgiveness you gave to the person who hurts you, to yourself.

forgiving yourself without regrets,

allowing it to have a sound rest

remember that the freedom to fly free and high

is open for you to possess.

Perhaps, it is deadliest to grieve someone who is still alive than you suffer those who are gone. My dad is just something unforgettable, but I know he will guide me through my *soul restoration*. I still look up to days when I'll sit under the sun without any worries, and things will not feel so bad.

Go laugh in the places you've once cried.

This day is allocated only for our family day. It doesn't come once a week. We need to lend our total energy to this moment. We have been so busy with our duties, and we tend to forget to feel the presence of everyone. My family is the precious thing I treasure the most. My dreams and aspirations will always be because of them and always be them.

Earthly stimuli might change us, yet our roots will remain solid. This makes us stick together. Despite everything, misunderstanding, and hatred built in your hearts in your family, reconciliation is always offered. *Keep seeking, and have an open heart.*

We took some photos together, a family picture. I may be lost for a while, but I am traveling my way home.

My home is my family that always got my back.

"Kakaiba talaga ang tikas ng pagkalalaki ng panganay niyo, daddy." My older brother said this to my father's tomb while letting our dad see the captured photo on his device. My Kuya is indeed sweet and handsome. The knight and shining armor dad left for my mom and me. He's smiling, and even so, I feel that he missed our father as I do. I want to hug Kuya tightly.

Hindi ko na ito nagawa dahil nagsalita ang aming bunso. "Mas guwapo kaya ang bunso, 'di ba, daddy and mommy? Cute pa, saka amoy baby."

"Yes sweetie, ikaw ang pinaka-guwapo sa kanila," ang sagot ni mom.

"Paamoy nga ng kilikili kung amoy baby oh," ang komento ko. Hindi na siya makakapagreklamo dahil tinapat ko na ang ilong ko sa kilikili niya at inamoy ito.

"Bakit amoy tatay na iyan?" I joke.

"Mommy, oh," my younger brother looked on our mom and pouted. He is a mama's boy indeed. No one is more handsome. My kuya and bunso ang pinaka-guwapong lalaki sa mga mata ko. *Lance is included, too.*

"Huwag ka ngang ganiyan kay bunso, Diko. Siya ang ating master," ang siya namang wika ni Kuya.

Although we have same look, mas nakuha ni Bunso ang wangis ng daddy namin. My dad was an airman. I still remember the first meet-up story they used to tell us while having a long drive. My mom then worked at the university where my dad was required to undergo professional training. My mom was one of the speakers at that time. Their eyes met, they eventually found a home, and they built a family together, so we're here, three. My Kuya is a scholar of the government; he's just finishing some units and will be a hot policeman soonest. Walang ginastos sa kaniya si mom simula ng nag-aral siya ng college. The government only pays back the sacrifices my dad served for this country.

I am just smiling throughout the typical conversation we used to have before. A usual one which makes you realize that this is life. No more begging of love because I am surrounded by people who won't be tired of loving me.

True love never lets you question yourself

true love answers all your queries

by empathic communication and genuine presence.

After almost 5 hours, we decided to go back home and watch a family movie together in our movie room. If you are familiar with the local film wherein the protagonists are four women, and their younger brother's getting married, this is the movie my mother selected for us to watch. The storytelling is not merely entertaining; the film itself is a masterpiece. I admire the resiliency of the mother in the movie. As a solo parent, she raised independent children who are fighters in life and who will choose their family above all.

I have been witnessing how hard to be a single mother because I have one. My mother is so strong that she is ready to fight any battle just for us to have a safe and better life. I know she sometimes wants to give up; however, she doesn't want us to experience the consequences of her decision.

Look at your mother,

you'll find the undying love

you're sailing to the wrong person.

She's the prettiest

among all the possession

you could have.

The movie is about to end, and my phone rings; Danica is calling. I do not want to answer her call for the first time, but it continues. I needed to answer it when it rang for the third time. I looked for space so I couldn't interrupt my family, who were having a good time.

'He's gone.'

The broken voice of Danica and her shivering message is enough to tell that something is not okay. There's something to be heard. Something I am not sure of.

'Sino?' ang naguguluhan kong tanong. Logic has been brought to the table. I know that someone plays a significant role in my life. Danica will not contact me

continuously if the subject of her call is just a stranger. Unti-unti na akong kinabahan.

'Him.'

Hindi ko pa man din natitiyak kung sino ang tinutukoy niya pero naghatid ito ng isang punyal na humiwa sa aking dibdib. Hatid nito ay sakit, sakit na akala ko ay 'di na mauulit pa. Kasinungalingan ang pag-aakala na ito ay naghilom na.

'Si Lance, na-aksidente siya habang pauwi sa kanila sa sobrang kalasingan.'

My tears are conditioned automatically. My cry gets my family's attention because one of them opens the light in the room. I saw their face looking up at me with confusion and mercy. Danica keeps talking, but my ears no longer accept words as my right hand becomes weak, and my phone falls to the ground.

After Five Days

TODAY will be my last day to see Lance. Until now, I could not believe that everything that happened was real. I thought it was just a nightmare I used to have after my father passed away. This time, *a disastrous nightmare comes into reality.*

Why does this world always want me to suffer? The men who made me feel that being gay is not a sin but a blessing that should be treasured and proud of always left me. Of course, I know that God is preparing me for something great. He wants to see me living the life he dreamt of when he created me. Hope is everywhere but along the way, God will put something that can hurt you, break you, and make you want to give up, only to see every situation as a blessing.

It is okay to suffer but do not allow suffering itself to destroy your precious gift, and that's your life.

I spent time standing at the white caffeine of my man. I may not have him, but he once owned me, and that *once is forever*. He looks like an angel. His face is calm, and he's smiling knowing he'll now be back in his original shelter. Be reunited with the **One** who made him.

As much as I desire to touch him, I feel powerless as I can't do that. A woman with a familiar psyche stands beside me. She is Lance's mother based on the pictures I saw on my man's phone.

"Thank you for loving my son during the days he didn't know how to love, even himself," she said.

I smiled at her then spoke. "***It's my choice*** to love your son. Even if he's gone, I will still always choose to love him until my soul lives."

The father who will bless Lance interrupted our conversation.

"As we pray for him, may his soul rest in ***eternal peace***."

About the Author

Edrian A. Diaz

Edrian A. Diaz is a passionate writer who weaves stories on various online writing platforms. Writing does not only feed his soul to keep it alive but it is also his bread and butter. He loves writing romantic-comedy stories which paved him to finish writing his first humorous-fantasy novel at the age of 16. He loves joining writing camps and workshops to master his craft. Edrian lives in San Rafael, Bulacan, Philippines, and spends his days studying BS Education. He also expresses his love of weaving words on his Instagram page: @*avante_ed*.